P9-AFW-977

Edgar Allan Poe's

Tales of Terror

Edgar Allan Poe's
Tales of Terror

Adapted by **Les Martin**

A STEPPING STONE BOOK™

Random House New York

This is a work of fiction. Names, characters, places, and incidents either are the product of the author's imagination or are used fictitiously. Any resemblance to actual persons, living or dead, events, or locales is entirely coincidental.

Copyright © 1991, 2007 by Random House, Inc.

All rights reserved. Published in the United States by Random House Children's Books, a division of Random House, Inc., New York. Originally published in different form by Random House Children's Books, a division of Random House, Inc., in 1991.

RANDOM HOUSE and colophon are registered trademarks and A STEPPING STONE BOOK and colophon are trademarks of Random House, Inc.

www.steppingstonesbooks.com
www.randomhouse.com/kids

Educators and librarians, for a variety of teaching tools, visit us at
www.randomhouse.com/teachers

Library of Congress Cataloging-in-Publication Data
Martin, Les.
Edgar Allan Poe's tales of terror / adapted by Les Martin.
    p.   cm.
"A Stepping Stone Book."
SUMMARY: Presents four chilling tales adapted for easy reading.
ISBN 978-0-375-84055-5 (pbk.) — ISBN 978-0-375-94055-2 (lib. bdg.)
1. Horror tales, American.   2. Children's stories, American. [1. Horror stories.   2. Short stories.] I. Poe, Edgar Allan, 1809–1849. Short stories. Selections.   II. Title: Tales of terror.
PZ7.M36353Ed   2007   [Fic]—dc22   2006022150

Printed in the United States of America
10 9 8 7 6 5 4 3 2

Contents

The Masque of the Red Death

A terrible sickness spread over the land. It was called the Red Death. Red is the color of blood. Blood oozing through every pore of the skin. That was the sign of the sickness and the seal of death.

All who caught it died within a half hour. But first they felt horrible pain and grew dizzy. Then they were stained red with their own blood.

With the Red Death came fear. No one was safe from the Death. And no one was safe from the fear.

No one, that is, except one man.

The great Prince Prospero ruled the land. He was the strongest of the strong. The bravest of the brave. The richest of the rich. The Red Death was mighty, but not as mighty as Prince Prospero. Fear might rule others, but not a ruler like him.

Let the Red Death rage everywhere. Let it turn farms into graveyards. Let it litter city streets with corpses. Let it slay workers at work, children in school. It could not touch Prince Prospero or those he chose to save.

Prince Prospero had many castles. But one was his favorite by far. He himself had drawn its plans. He had made sure the builders followed them. The castle was perfect down to the last detail. It was like a mirror of the prince's mind. It reflected everything he desired.

The prince now went to this castle. With him came the flower of his royal court. The boldest knights. The most beautiful ladies. Musicians, ballet dancers, jugglers, and clowns to amuse them. And servants to care for their every want and need.

All told, a thousand people came with Prospero. The castle was more than large enough for them. And easily able to feed them. Storerooms held food for years of feasting. Trees in the gardens bore fruit for every season. A spring brought fresh water from deep in the earth. Vast cellars were filled with the finest wines.

A wall around the castle stood above

all. The highest, thickest wall that could be built.

Only one door led through this wall. A door of solid iron. The door was locked as soon as the prince and his followers entered. But he was not satisfied with even this. He ordered it sealed shut. Sealed with molten metal. It hardened in an hour. The door was airtight.

No one could enter the castle now. No matter how desperate to escape the Red Death. And no one could leave. Not even anyone insane enough to risk it.

The people inside the castle had no choice. They could only enjoy themselves all day and night.

The people outside had no choice either. They could only wait for the Red Death to strike at any time.

All those lucky people inside the castle hailed the prince. He had won out over the Red Death. Here in his castle they would live until the Red Death died out. Then the whole land would be theirs. Theirs alone.

But Prince Prospero could not rest long on his victory. In a few months he faced a new enemy. An enemy within his castle and within his very being. An enemy he had to overcome.

Boredom.

It grew stronger with every passing day. Every week. Every month.

Boredom attacked the prince. It attacked his followers. The most delicious food tasted stale. The rarest wines seemed sour. Clowns drew groans. Jugglers drew yawns.

Finally, Prince Prospero gathered his followers before him.

"I invite you to a party," he said. "A celebration. We have been in the castle six months now. Six months of safety. Six months of pleasure. The best six months of our lives. So I want to make this the best party ever."

The party would be a masque, the prince told them. A masked ball—with everyone in costumes. Anyone could come as anything. And could do anything. At this party anything went. The wilder the better.

And there would be a special treat. The masque would be in Prospero's private rooms. Only trusted servants had seen them before. Now everyone would enjoy them.

There was no boredom in the castle that week. Brains and fingers worked overtime to create strange costumes. Tongues wagged about what Prospero's private rooms were like. The great prince had designed them himself. They had to be very original.

The prince's followers were not disappointed.

The night of the party they poured into the prince's rooms. Eagerly they explored them.

All the doors between the rooms were open, but each room was a separate surprise. The prince had not laid out his rooms in a straight line. Each room was at a sharp angle to the one before it. A guest could see only one room at a time. With no hint of what came next.

The first room was all blue. The vivid blue of an autumn sky. The furniture was blue. The walls and ceiling were blue. A blue carpet covered the floor. And tall blue windows faced each other on two sides.

The only light in the room came from outside the windows. There, fires blazed in metal stands. The blue windows turned the firelight blue. That blue light bathed the blue of the room.

The second room was all purple. The purple of kings, bathed in purple light.

The next one, the green of great lawns.

Next, the orange of flames.

After that, the blinding white of snow.

Then came the violet of a dazzling sunset.

But nothing prepared a guest for the

seventh room. No one could escape its shock.

The room was black. The deepest black. The black of a bottomless hole.

Except for the windows.

They were blood-red. Blood-red light came through them and cast hideous shadows.

Guests shrank from that light. Quickly they left. Few stayed long enough to see the clock in the room. A towering black clock. But all heard it. It chimed ominously every hour.

That sound went through every room. It cut through the music. Through the talk. Through the laughter. It was like a sudden chill.

But when the sound died, the party fever rose again. The party went on, even wilder than before. It was as if everyone had forgotten the clock would chime again. The frightening feeling would return.

The prince walked among his guests. He was pleased. He had told them to enjoy themselves, and they were obeying his command.

He smiled to see them dancing. Laughing. Drinking. Their voices grew louder and louder. Their feet more and more clumsy.

Above all, he was amused by their costumes. He had urged his guests to set no limits on their imagination. They had obeyed. He saw gods and devils, clowns and animals. He saw kings and beggars, policemen and thieves. The divine and the horrible. He saw everything men and women could dream of being.

Then the party paused again. The black clock was chiming. Twelve times. Midnight had come.

The last chime died away. Music and laughter rose. The prince looked across the blue room. There he saw the strangest costume of all, and his smile faded.

The person wearing the costume stood alone. The costume filled other guests with disgust and horror.

The figure was tall and thin. Its costume was a shroud. A corpse's shroud that hung from head to feet. Its mask was just as gruesome. A chalk-white mask that was a perfect copy of a corpse's face. But even this was not the worst of it. The mask was spotted with bright dots of red.

This guest had come as a victim of the Red Death.

The prince's face grew pale with shock. And with a swift, sudden touch of fear.

Then it grew red with rage.

He would not let this hideous joke spoil his perfect party.

"Who dares insult us?" he roared to his followers. "Seize him. Unmask him. So we can know who he is before we hang him at sunrise."

Prince Prospero's commanding voice rang through all the rooms. His followers moved to seize the strange figure.

But the figure did not retreat. Instead it advanced with a slow, solemn step. Straight toward the prince.

The prince's followers parted before it. They gave the figure a clear path. A stab of fear went through them. The same icy fear that had touched the prince himself.

Frozen, they watched the figure pass by the prince. Within a yard of him.

Prince Prospero was frozen, too. He watched the figure leave the blue room.

Then again a wave of hot anger flooded through the prince. Anger at this man who mocked his power. And anger at his own moment of weakness.

His followers might bow to fear. That was why they *were* followers. But he could not surrender to it. That was why they bowed to him.

Raging, the prince rushed into the purple room. But the figure had left. It had gone on to the next room.

In the green room the story was the same. And in the orange. The white. The violet. The figure kept its lead.

Prince Prospero was not worried. The

figure was in the black room now. From that room there was no escape. Not from the prince. And not from the dagger in his hand.

The prince raised his dagger high. His eyes gleamed. The gleam of a hunter closing in on his prey. He entered the black room and saw he had his prey trapped.

The shrouded figure was at the far end of the room. Its back was toward the prince. Prince Prospero rushed toward it.

Then the figure turned.

The prince was four feet away.

He got no farther.

A sharp cry came from his mouth.

The dagger dropped from his hand. It fell on the black carpet.

Then the prince fell. Fell to lie beside his dagger.

His body lay facedown on the black carpet. It lay there still as a corpse. Bathed in the red light.

His followers saw all this through the open doorway. Their love and loyalty overcame fear. They poured into the room, ready to tear the motionless shrouded figure apart.

But all they found was an empty shroud that had crumpled to the floor. Beside it lay the chalk-white mask. Right in front of the towering black clock. The clock that had now stopped.

Then they turned the prince over and saw his face bathed in the blood-red light. But it was no trick of light they saw. It was blood as red as the light.

Now they knew who had come to their party.

Now they knew who had come un-invited, like a thief in the night.

Now they knew who was among them, touching them all.

One by one they fell to the floor. Writhing. Howling in pain. In the black room. The violet. The white. The orange. The green. The purple. The blue. And in every room their blood stained the carpets.

One by one the flames outside the windows went out. In the black room. The violet. The white. The orange. The green. The purple. The blue.

Until darkness ruled the castle.

Darkness—and the Red Death.

The Cask of Amontillado

How I hated Fortunato! For more reasons than I can tell.

He had tricked me out of money. Forced me to sell land. Stolen the girl I loved. Laughed in my face. Insulted me. And far worse, insulted my noble family. Imagine a pig like him insulting the noble Montresors!

That was the last straw. That I could never forgive.

How I longed to do the simple thing. Plunge a dagger into him or run him through with my sword.

But "the simple thing" would not do. The law would take my life in return. Fortunato had to pay for all he had done. But pay with *his* life alone, not *mine*.

One thing more. It was not enough to make Fortunato pay. He had to *know* he was paying. He could not die still looking down his nose at me. Still thinking he was better than a Montresor. No! Never!

Settling the score with Fortunato would not be easy. I needed time. Time to think. To plan. To find the right moment. The right place. The right way.

At last I made my plans. I was careful not to put him on guard. I smiled when he teased me about losing my fortune and love. I laughed at his jokes about my family while I waited for the right time to come.

Fortunato and I lived in a town in the north of Italy. Lent—the forty days before Easter—is a time of fasting and prayer. A dull, dreary time. Is it any wonder that before Lent begins, the people here have a festival? Some call it Mardi Gras. Others, Carnival.

It is a week of madness and gaiety. People dress up in costumes. Have parades. Give parties. Dance. Sing. And drink.

Above all, they drink. Our part of Italy is fond of wine and boasts of drinking the very best.

In our town no one liked wine more than Fortunato or claimed to know wine so well. Indeed I must admit that he was an expert. A true expert.

That was why his eyes lit up at my story, as I knew they would.

His eyes were already bright with wine. It was the last night of Carnival. Fortunato wore the costume of a jester. Red tights on his thin legs. Clothes of many colors on his fat body. And a cap with jingling bells on his head.

"My dear Fortunato," I said, putting my hand warmly on his shoulder. "How well you look! And how lucky for me to run into you in this crowd. You're the one man who can help me."

"How so?" he asked. But he was already looking around him. He was eager to get rid of me. And to go on to the next party.

My hand stayed on his shoulder. "No one else has your taste in wine. You see, I have just bought a truly fine wine. Fresh Amontillado. A cask of it at a very low price. So low that I was afraid of letting it get away. But now I'm afraid I was tricked."

I had Fortunato's attention now.

"Amontillado!" He chuckled. "You can't get fresh Amontillado this time of year!"

"That is why I have my doubts," I said.

"Amontillado!" he repeated. His laughter brought tears to his eyes.

"And I must satisfy those doubts," I went on. "I was on my way to see Luchesi when I ran into you. I wanted him to taste the wine. And to tell me if it really is Amontillado."

"Luchesi!" Fortunato sneered. "He could not tell Amontillado from tea."

"Yet some fools say his taste is as good

as yours," I said. I knew I had hit the right note.

"Surely even *you* are not that big a fool," Fortunato said. At that moment he started coughing. He had a cold.

I waited for his coughing to stop.

"I would have gone to you," I told him. "But I knew how busy you are at Carnival. You are so popular. So much in demand. That is why I decided to ask Luchesi. He would never turn down free wine. Especially if it really might be Amontillado."

Fortunato grabbed me by the arm. "Come, let us go," he said.

"Where?" I asked.

"To your *so-called* Amontillado," Fortunato said.

"I can't take you away from all your friends," I protested.

"But you are my friend, too, aren't you?" Fortunato said.

"Of course I am," I declared. "Among your best, I hope."

"Then it is my duty as a friend to help you," Fortunato said.

"No, I can't let you do it," I said firmly.

"Why not?" Fortunato demanded.

"The Amontillado is in my wine cellar," I said. "It is cold and damp down there. You have a cold already. This would make it worse."

"Nonsense," Fortunato said. His voice was harsh and strong. The voice of a man who always got his way. "This cold is nothing. Besides, I will find wine to warm my blood. Your cellar is famous."

"My family has stored wine there for centuries," I agreed. "Wine to delight even an expert like you."

Fortunato and I crossed the town square. It was packed with people dancing and drinking. I was wearing a black cape with a hood. I had lowered a black silk mask over my face. Nobody noticed me.

Now and then someone called out to Fortunato. But he did not stop. He had gleaming eyes only for my house. My family home. The mansion of the Montresors.

It was deserted. I had told my servants I would be out all night. I then ordered them not to leave the house for Carnival. I was sure they would do the opposite as soon as my back was turned. And they had.

Fortunato looked around as we went through the house. At the paintings. The suits of armor. The antiques. The Oriental rugs. Perhaps he was scheming how to take it from me. Knowing Fortunato, he probably was.

I took two flaming torches from their holders. One for Fortunato and one for me. We went down the winding stone steps to the cellar. I warned him to be careful.

When we reached the bottom of the steps, Fortunato's eyes widened.

"Your wine cellar is large," he said.

"This is more than a wine cellar," I told him. "It also serves as my family burial place. As you can see."

Fortunato nodded uneasily. My "cellar" was a wide underground passageway. It was cut through solid rock. Along the sides were wine racks. But there were also shelves cut into the sides. Shelves that held coffins—and skeletons. The bones of the Montresors.

"What is that ugly white stuff over everything?" asked Fortunato. He pointed at the white crust on the rock. On the coffins. Even on the wine bottles. It looked like salt.

"It is saltpeter," I explained. "The dampness makes it seep from the rock. The cold makes it harden. I warned you how cold and damp it is down here."

At that moment Fortunato began to cough. His whole body shook.

"My dear friend, let us go back," I said.

"Forget the Amontillado. Your health is precious. You are rich, loved, and admired. A man to be missed. Let Luchesi catch a chill down here."

Fortunato forced himself to stop coughing.

"Nonsense!" he snapped. "A little cough will not kill me."

"No," I agreed. "A cough will not kill you. Here, take a drink of this to wet your throat."

I opened a bottle of rare Medoc wine. Fortunato took a deep drink. The bells on his cap jingled.

"I drink to the dead that rest around us," said Fortunato.

"And I drink to your long life," I said.

Fortunato's wine-stained tongue licked his fat lips. He was no longer shivering.

But his walk was weaving as we went down the passageway.

The passageway led to another. And another. The crust of saltpeter grew thicker. The air grew colder. Damper. More stale. So that our torches burned ever more dimly. Still we went on.

"Where is this Amontillado?" Fortunato grumbled. "At the end of the earth?"

"Not quite," I said. "But I told you this cellar is large. So many are buried here."

"Ah, yes. Your family," said Fortunato. His lips curled. "The noble Montresors. Tell me, what is your coat of arms? I forget."

"A huge human foot of gold in a field of blue," I said. "The foot is crushing a snake. While the snake's fangs are biting the heel."

"And the motto?" asked Fortunato.

"'No one who angers me goes unpunished,'" I told him.

"Very good," said Fortunato. He started to chuckle. But a fit of coughing cut his laughter off. I opened another bottle for him.

"Try this," I said. "It is even better than the first."

He drank eagerly, and he wiped his mouth with the back of his hand.

"Excellent," he said. Then he made a strange gesture with his hand.

I looked at him, puzzled.

He made the sign again.

When he saw that I did not understand, he said, "It is a sign of the Masons. The secret society that I belong to. I wanted to see if you were one of us."

I smiled. "But I am. This is my sign," I said. From under my cloak I took a mason's trowel.

It was Fortunato's turn to look puzzled. Then he smiled. "Ah, a joke. You surprise me. You do have a little wit at least."

He took another long swig. He threw the empty bottle against the wall. The broken glass fell among bones piled there.

"Not all your family had coffins," he said.

"There were many Montresors," I said. "Generations and generations of Montresors and their servants. And others as well."

"Along with all this wonderful wine," said Fortunato. He looked at the high wine racks. His eyes still shone. But now through a mist. A mist of drink. His voice was blurred, too. "But where is the Amontillado?"

"Not far," I assured him.

Fortunato's walk was even more unsteady now. I gripped his arm to keep him from stumbling.

"Maybe we should go back," I said again. "Feel how cold it is getting. Feel how damp the rock is. Luchesi can—"

"Forget Luchesi!" Fortunato bellowed. "The Amontillado!"

"Yes, the Amontillado," I said.

The passageway sloped downward through one archway after another. The archways were lower and lower. The saltpeter was thicker, too. It hung like cobwebs everywhere. Bones were piled along the walls up to the curved ceiling.

"We've reached it," I announced.

I pointed to the end of the passageway lined with skeletons. There was a low arch. There was a pile of bones in front of it. Beyond the arch a final room had been cut into the rock.

"At last the Amontillado," Fortunato growled hoarsely.

"Yes, the Amontillado," I said.

Fortunato broke into a staggering run. The bells on his cap jingled. He reached the archway before me. He stuck his torch into the room, but it no longer was flaming. His torch gave off only a feeble glow. He could not see where the room ended.

"Go in," I said. I followed close behind.

"The Amontillado! Where is it?" Fortunato demanded. He had reached a bare rock wall. Puzzled, he stared at it.

He did not notice the iron rings in the

rock. Or the chain hanging from one of them. And the padlock on the other.

I did not give him time to notice.

Swiftly I passed the chain tight around his body. Then I fastened it with the padlock.

I pulled the key out of the lock and stepped back to the archway.

"Feel the rock, dear friend," I said. "How damp it is. How cold. I beg you once more. Let us return. No? You won't? Then I must leave you. But first I will do you one last favor. I will make sure no one disturbs you while you enjoy the Amontillado."

"The Amontillado!" said Fortunato. He shook his drunken head dully. He still did not know what was happening.

"Yes, the Amontillado," I said as I pushed aside a pile of bones.

Behind them was a heap of large build-ing stones. There was cement as well. I used wine instead of water to mix the cement. Then I set to work with my trowel. I laid a row of stones across the entrance to the room.

I heard a signal that the wine was wear-ing off Fortunato. There was a low moan-ing cry. It was not the cry of a drunken man.

Then there was silence. Stubborn silence. Or perhaps hopeless silence.

I kept on working. I laid a row of stones on top of the first row. Then another. And another.

At that point I heard the chain loudly clanking. He must have been desperately trying to break it. Or tear it free from the wall.

I stopped to better enjoy the sounds. I sat down on a pile of bones to listen to the noise. It was like listening to music.

The clanking ended. I went back to work. I finished the fifth row. The sixth. The seventh. The wall was as high as my chest now.

I paused again. I thrust my torch over the wall. I could dimly see Fortunato's chained figure.

Screams burst from his throat. Hideous screams. One after another.

I stiffened. I retreated. My hand went to the hilt of my sword. Then my other hand touched the rock side of the passageway. I felt how solid it was. How strong. I thought of the iron rings in the rock. The rings that Fortunato was trying to pull out. I relaxed.

I returned to my unfinished wall. I answered Fortunato's screams with my own. My screams were louder and stronger. He was quiet by the time I stopped.

I laid the eighth row of stones. The ninth. The tenth. Almost all of the eleventh. The last row.

By now it was midnight. The wall reached the ceiling. There was a single gap left. I just had to put one large stone in place. Then cement it.

It was heavy. Panting, I lifted it. I moved it partway into the gap. Then I heard laughter. It made my hair stand on end.

It was followed by a sad voice. A voice that did not sound like Fortunato at all.

"Ha, ha, ha!" it croaked. "What a clever joke. You are a witty fellow. I am sorry for ever thinking the opposite. We'll have a good laugh about it back at Carnival. Over a good bottle of wine."

"Yes," I said. "Over the Amontillado."

"He, he, he!" Fortunato cackled. "Right. Over the Amontillado. But it's getting late. People will wonder where we are. My wife will start worrying. Let us be gone."

"Yes," I said. "Let us be gone."

"For the love of God, Montresor!" Fortunato shrieked.

"Yes," I said. "For the love of God."

I waited for him to say more. But there was nothing.

"Fortunato!" I called.

No answer.

"Fortunato!" I called again.

Still no answer.

I thrust my torch through the hole. It barely fit through the gap. I let it drop into the room.

I heard only the jingling of bells. The bells on Fortunato's fool's cap.

Suddenly I began to feel a little ill. Because of the dampness, no doubt.

I hurried to cement the last stone into place. Then I piled old bones against the new wall. They covered it completely.

That was half a century ago.

The bones have not been disturbed.

Fortunato, rest in peace!

The Tell-Tale Heart

They say I am mad. Do not believe it.
I am sane. Totally sane and intelligent.
Highly intelligent. Of course, like all
highly intelligent people, I am sensitive—
very sensitive.

Take my sense of hearing. My hearing
above all. Drop a pin and I will hear it.
But my other senses are keen as well. My
sense of sight, for instance. I see things

that most people cannot. Otherwise the old man still would be alive.

You see, on the surface, I had every reason to like him. He was always sunny and smiling. He would try to brighten my darkest moods. He was kind and understanding. He never questioned my complaints about the world. He charged me no rent for my room in his house, asking only for help with heavy chores. Indeed, when I could not sell my writing, he offered to lend me money. Not that I would take it—especially when I looked into his eye.

His eye, I say, for he had only one, with a black patch over the other. It was a pale blue eye. Even now, I can close my eyes and see it. A film coated that eye like a shimmering teardrop. But that coating could not hide his pity. I could see it plain as my face in the mirror.

It was easy to see why he looked down on me. He was rich and I was poor. He had known success in life and I knew only failure. I could understand his scorn—but I could not forgive it. I had to make him pay for it. But more than that, I had to wipe that scorn from his eye. He had to see me as I really was. He had to look up to me. He had to die with his cursed eye open.

Each day I answered the old man's smile with my own. Each day I returned his kindness with my own. Each morning I asked if he had slept well. Each bedtime I wished him pleasant dreams. And each night at midnight I opened his bedroom door. I opened it slowly, silently, and carefully.

Night after night I did this. You see, practice makes perfect, and mine would be the perfect crime.

As I said, each midnight I opened his door. I opened it just wide enough for my head to poke through. In my hand was a lantern. It was lit but covered with cloth. I thrust the lantern into the room. I parted the cloth so that a single ray of light fell on the old man in bed. I moved the light to fall on the eye I hated. But for seven nights that eye remained closed. And it had to be open to see me when I struck. Everything had to be perfect.

On the eighth night, I opened the door more slowly than ever. Never had I felt so powerful. The old man did not dream what I was doing—and would do. I almost chuckled at his blindness and my brilliance.

Maybe I did chuckle. Maybe he heard me. I do not know. I only know I heard him stir in bed.

But this did not stop me. Tonight nothing could stop me. Tonight everything felt perfect.

I had my head in the room and was about to shine the lantern when a second sound reached my ears. It was the rustle of the old man rising from bed. Then came a quavering cry, *"Who's there?"*

I froze. For an hour I did not move. It was not hard to stand so still. Quite the reverse. I enjoyed every moment. It was like letting ice cream slowly melt on my tongue. I wanted to make it last. It was delicious to picture the old man trembling in the dark.

He would tell himself it was nothing. He had heard the wind in the chimney. Or maybe a mouse had run across the floor. His shivering would not stop. He could not see my head in the doorway, but he could *feel* it. He could feel a growing chill—the chill of death coming closer. I could picture this, for I myself have had this waking nightmare. I have had it all too often.

After an hour, I still had not heard him lie down. He, like me, was frozen, but he was frozen with fear.

It was I who moved first. Ever so slightly, I parted the cloth on the lantern. The thinnest of rays shot out. Like an arrow hitting the center of a target, it fell on the old man's pale blue eye.

Still I did not move. That glistening eye held me in its spell. It seemed to drain the blood from my body. Then I heard the sound a ticking watch might make.

At first it was muffled, as if the watch were wrapped in cotton. Only someone with my sharp hearing could hear it. I not only heard it, I knew what it was. It was the beating of the old man's heart.

It did not frighten me. Not in the least. In fact, it made my own heart quicken. It was like a drum calling me to battle. My body tensed. My muscles swelled. I ached to spring into action.

Still I paused. I wanted to let this force fill me from head to toe.

But the beating kept getting louder. Louder and louder. Soon neighbors would hear it. I had to stop it. Already it was so loud that I could barely hear my own yell as I ripped the cover off the lantern. I could barely hear the old man scream as I charged into the room. He was still screaming as my fingers found his throat.

Grunting, I choked that scream off. As my fingers tightened, the beating grew fainter. I smiled. Only *I* could hear it now. I gave a final squeeze. The beating stopped. I put my hand on the old man's chest. I held it there a full minute. There was no movement. He was stone dead.

Joy washed over me. The joy of victory. But I did not lose my head.

I carried the old man into the bathroom and laid him in the tub.

Hours later, my task was done. The old man's body lay in pieces in the space below the bedroom floor.

I replaced the boards so perfectly that no one could see they had been disturbed.

I washed the tub so that not a trace of blood remained.

Finally, I straightened the bed coverings.

Such care took time. I heard a church bell strike four. No matter. I could sleep late. And I could sleep well.

Bone tired, I returned to my room. I put on my nightclothes. I lay down in bed and pulled up the covers. Then I heard a knocking on the front door of the house.

Instantly I was wide awake. I felt my heart racing. But I made myself move slowly. I took my time going to the door. I made a show of rubbing sleep from my eyes when I opened it.

Three policemen stood there.

Was anything the matter? I asked. My voice dripped with respect.

The police were just as polite. They hated to bother me. But a passerby had reported a noise in the night. It might have been a scream. It might have come from this house. They had to look into it. Could they come in?

Another person might have shown fear. Not I. I welcomed them. In the hallway I faced them without flinching. I answered their questions without a stutter.

No, I had heard no noise.

Yes, I was in the house alone.

No, I was not the owner.

The owner was on a trip to Europe. He was in poor health and looking for a cure.

I was here to look after his property.

The policemen nodded. They were ready to believe me. They were ready to go.

A weaker man might have let them leave, but not I. I would not let them go so quickly. I had waited too long for a chance like this. It was my chance to mock the world that had mocked me for so long. These stupid fools would not cut it short. I would play them for fools a bit longer. I would leave no doubt who was the better man.

Maybe there had been a noise, I told them. Thieves might have broken into the apartment. The owner had valuables in his bedroom. Perhaps thieves were still lurking there. Would the officers come with me to make sure everything was all right?

I led the police to the bedroom. I was

careful not to let them see the triumph in my eyes.

I took a seat as the police searched the room. I sat there watching them like a king on a throne. Even better, to add spice to this moment, my chair was directly over the remains of the old man.

The police finished their work. They found nothing wrong. Yet they seemed in no hurry to go.

A slight chill went through me. It was time for them to go. Why did they linger here?

It was cold out, I reasoned. They might be waiting for me to offer them coffee or something stronger. Or perhaps they simply were lazy and wanted a long break from work. There had to be many reasons why they stayed and chatted about crime in the neighborhood and the importance of staying alert.

Well, let them stay as long as they wanted. They would not see a trace of worry or weakness in me. I listened to them and agreed with them without a hint of nerves.

But as they stayed and stayed, and talked and talked, my head began to ache. Still I kept smiling and nodding at their chatter. Even when a faint ringing started in my head, I gave nothing away. If anything, I smiled and nodded even more. I made my own voice rise above the ringing as I joined in their talk. Talk of sports, of politics, of families, of the weather. Talk that would drive the sanest of men mad.

And all the while, the sound in my head grew louder.

I could no longer sit still. I had to move to clear my mind.

I rose to my feet, still talking. I punched my fist into my palm to show how strongly I felt about what I was saying. But what was I saying? I hardly knew. The sound was drowning all else out.

I realized then that the sound was not in my mind. It came from outside. And I could no longer mistake it for ringing.

It was the sound a ticking watch might make.

I knew that sound. It was muffled now—the sound of a watch wrapped in cotton. But it would grow louder. It would grow clearer. You would not mistake it for a watch ticking. You would know it was a heart beating. Beating, beating, beating.

I raised my voice even more, but it was too late. Already that beating was louder than my voice. Louder than anything short of a scream.

The police showed no sign of being disturbed. In fact, they were smiling as they talked.

I could not follow what they were saying. All I could hear was the beating. But their smiles told me more than words could. They were smiles of silent laughter. The police were laughing at me. Laughing at me for pretending nothing was wrong. Laughing at me as they let me go on and on. Laughing at me as if I were a clown. I was not playing them for fools. They were playing with me. Playing with me the way a cat plays with a mouse.

Of course they heard the beating. They *had* to hear it. By now it was deafening. The walls seemed to shake with it. My head was splitting. But those mocking smiles were worse. They were like knives cutting into me. Cutting me to pieces.

I could stand it no longer. The beating was too loud. The smiles were too cruel.

I had to stop this torture.

I had to stop it before it drove me mad.

"You monsters!" I screamed. "You fiends! You win! I confess! Tear up these planks! Look under them! You will find it there! You will find that hideously beating heart!"

The Pit and the Pendulum

"*You are condemned to death!*"

I heard no more. Not how I was to die. Nor when. Nor where.

I already knew why I was to die. I was an agent of France. The new France. The France of the Revolution. The France of Napoleon. The France that wanted to free all Europe from the chains of the past.

And this was Spain, where the king

hated France and freedom. And where the Church hated them even more.

The Holy Inquisition was the unholy weapon of that hate. I sat before its judges. Their robes were jet-black. Their faces were deathly white. Their thin lips seemed as white as the paper I now write upon. I saw no pity on those faces. I watched their white lips moving.

"You are condemned to death."

As I said, I heard no more. Not even my name. I felt sick. Sick as death. I looked away from those white faces. Those white lips. I gazed at the candles on the judges' table. Seven tall white candles. They seemed to turn into slender white angels. Angels who would save me. Then that picture faded. And I saw only the cruel flames.

I did not see them long. Those flames vanished. Vanished into blackness. I had fainted. Fainted dead away.

I was dead to the world. It was like sleep. Dreams came and went. Some pleasant. Others nightmares. Some filled with people and places I knew. Others with things I had never seen before. Some bright with hope. Others dark with despair.

Then the dreams stopped. All was blackness and silence. Except for a single sound. My heart beating.

I was awake. But my mind was empty. And my eyes were shut tight.

I was afraid to open my eyes. I was afraid even to think.

But thoughts came on their own. Memories.

I remembered being captured. I was

tied up hand and foot. I was taken to the city of Toledo. The fortress of the Inquisition.

I remembered the joke of a trial. The black-robed judges. Their white lips moving.

"You are condemned to death."

But what happened to me after that?

I dreaded to see what might be around me. At last I forced my eyes open. And saw—nothing.

I was in blackness darker than any night. Blackness that pressed down like a heavy weight.

A horrible thought struck me. The Inquisition burned most of its victims at the stake. Quickly. Without delay.

Yet here I was. Where, I did not know. But I did know one thing. I was still alive.

But did *they* know? Or had they made a mistake? *Had they buried me alive?*

Cold sweat covered me. It stood in little beads on my forehead. What if I lay in my own tomb? I was afraid to find out. Yet I had to.

I rose to my feet. I was still afraid to take a step. Instead I waved my arms wildly around me in every direction. They touched nothing. If this was a tomb, at least it was large.

I slowly moved forward. My eyes felt as if they would pop out of my head. But they could not see even a hint of light.

I kept my arms in front of me. I took a few more steps and began to breathe easier. This was no tomb. I was in an underground cell. A dungeon—a dungeon of the Inquisition.

I recalled stories I had heard. Stories about the dungeons of the Inquisition. Of prisoners left to starve in them. Or to die of thirst.

But those stories were not the worst. There were other tales. Tales told in whispers about tortures that made death seem sweet.

My hand touched something in front of me. A wall. Very smooth, slimy, and cold.

I decided to find out the size of my cell. I would follow the wall around it. But first I had to mark my starting place.

I reached for my pocketknife. I found that my own clothes had been taken from me. A rough prisoner's robe replaced them. I tore a strip of cloth from the robe.

I put down the cloth next to the wall.

Then I started moving. Slowly. Carefully. Counting my steps. With one hand sliding along the smooth, slimy wall.

But I did not make it all the way around. The dungeon was larger than I thought. The ground was wet and slippery, and I was very weak. I stumbled and fell. Too tired to move, I lay there.

Sleep overcame me. When I awoke, my hand touched something. A loaf of bread. Then a pitcher of water. I wolfed down both.

Only then did I pause to think. The Inquisition was keeping track of me. It did not want me to starve to death. It wanted another kind of death for me. I shivered at the possibilities.

I continued following the wall. I had taken fifty-two steps before I went to sleep. I took forty-eight more. Then I reached my marker. The dungeon was a hundred steps around. There were about two steps to a yard. That made the room fifty yards around. A huge space.

But I wanted to know still more. The walls had many strange angles. I could not be sure of the dungeon's shape.

To get a better idea, I had to walk across it. I hated to leave the wall. But there was no other way.

I took a deep breath. I moved through the blackness boldly. For twelve steps.

Then suddenly I was falling.

I had tripped over my long robe. I hit the floor hard.

My head spun with the shock.

After a moment, my mind calmed. Then it froze.

I realized something was wrong. Very wrong.

My chin was resting against the floor.

But the rest of my head was tilted downward. And my mouth, nose, and forehead were touching nothing.

Nothing but clammy air. Air filled with a foul odor of decay.

I put my arm forward and reached down. My fingers closed on empty air.

I was lying at the edge of a circular pit. I had no idea how wide or deep it was. My hand felt along its edge. I found a loose piece of stone and pulled it free. Then I let it drop.

I listened. I heard it bouncing along the sides of the hole. It seemed to fall forever. Then at last I heard a very distant splash.

At that moment there was a gleam of light. It vanished as quickly as it came. A door had opened high above me. Then slammed shut.

The Inquisition had seen I was still alive. It knew I had escaped the pit.

But the Inquisition was not done with me. It still had me in its clutches. To play with as a cat plays with a caged bird. The Inquisition was expert at tortures of the body and tortures of the mind.

I knew how angry the Inquisition must be. Even angrier than before.

I had defied its power yet again. It would make me pay for that. I could only fear its next move. Fear it to the bottom of my soul.

My whole body was shaking. I felt my

way back to the wall. I vowed not to budge from it. Who knew how many deadly holes waited in the dark?

Hours slowly passed. I tried to keep awake. To stay on guard. But my eyelids grew too heavy. I drifted into sleep.

When I awoke, I found fresh bread and water by my hand. I was not hungry. But my throat burned with thirst. I grabbed the water pitcher and drank every drop in it.

It must have been drugged. Before long I was sleepy again. Very, very sleepy. I did not even try to fight it. I plunged into a deep, deep sleep.

I do not know how long I slept. But when I awoke the second time, everything had changed.

For one thing, there was light. A strange glow. I could not see at first from where it came. But for the first time I could see my cell.

I was shocked. It was far smaller than I had thought. Only about twenty-five yards around. I had made a mistake in measuring it.

This bothered me. Bothered me terribly. I needed to trust the power of my mind. It was all I had to save me. I had to figure out how I went wrong.

I forced myself to remember just what I had done. I had measured halfway around the wall. Then I had fallen asleep. I must have still been groggy when I woke up. Confused. I had started measuring again, but in the wrong direction. Back the way I had come. That accounted for the mistake. The difference between fifty yards and twenty-five.

I breathed easier. My mind was still working well. I went back to examining the cell.

The walls were also different than I had thought. They were not smooth, slimy plaster. They were metal. Probably iron. Put together in large plates. I recalled the angles I had felt. They were where the metal plates joined.

One thing I could not have guessed in the dark. The walls were covered with paintings. Pictures of fiends. Devils. Goblins. Skeletons. And every other form fear could take.

And, of course, I now could see something else. The most fearful sight of all. In the center of the stone floor.

The pit.

But one thing I could not do. I could not look down into it.

For I could not move anything but my head. That and my left arm.

I lay on my back on top of a low, narrow wood platform. A leather strap tied me down. It was wound around and around me like a bandage.

As I said, my left arm was free. With it I tested the strap. The leather was strong. Tight. I could find no way to get loose.

I turned my head. I saw why my left arm was free. A food dish had been put just within reach.

I had not been hungry before. But now I was starving. I reached the dish with difficulty. Then I grabbed at the food. I stuffed it into my mouth. I chewed and swallowed it.

It was some kind of meat. Lamb or mutton. Oily and salty. Very salty.

The salt made me unbearably thirsty. I looked for a water pitcher. To my horror there was none.

The Inquisition had begun a new torture. But worse was to come.

I stared up at the ceiling. It was at least forty feet high. It too was made of metal plates. There was a painting on one of them. It drew my gaze like a magnet.

I saw a picture of Father Time. He carried a scythe. The long, curved blade that farmers swing to cut their wheat. Father Time, of course, uses his scythe in another way. To cut lives short.

I looked more closely at the scythe in the painting. Its edge was pointed toward me. Suddenly my eyes bulged. *The scythe had moved!*

I stared even harder. There was no doubt of it. The curved blade was swinging. The scythe was not part of the painting. It was real. It hung below the painting like the pendulum of a grandfather clock. The pendulum is the weight that swings from side to side to keep the clock ticking.

For a while I watched it. Its swing was very short. Very slow. I was almost hypnotized.

Then a sound made me turn my head. I heard scurrying feet and a hideous chirping.

Rats were coming out of the hole. Big rats. Their hungry eyes gleaming. Their noses quivering.

They smelled the food in my dish. I waved my hand to scare them away. At first it was easy. But then they began to lose their fear. They crept closer. I had to wave harder.

This went on for almost an hour. My arm ached. I had to rest. I laid my head back. Again I looked upward.

What I saw made me forget the rats.

The curved blade still swung like a pendulum. But the swing was wider. And faster.

More important, *the blade was closer than before!*

Now I could see how large it was. How heavy. I could see its razor-sharp edge gleaming. And I could hear it. A horrible hissing as it swung through the air.

I tried to turn my eyes away. I could not. I tried to close them. I could not. They were held by the gleaming blade.

Its swing was wider each time. Faster. Louder. And closer.

But only a little closer each time. A tiny, tiny bit closer. If only it would come down faster! I began to pray it would. But the Inquisition was in no hurry. Those masters of torture were in no hurry to end my agony.

Hour after hour I lay there counting the movements of the pendulum. The hissing was ear-splitting. By now I could *smell* the steel blade. And I could see where it was aimed.

It would slice straight across my chest. Right through my heart.

Then a strange thing happened. Something the Inquisition had not planned. Something I did not expect.

One can get tired of anything—even fear. For a while, at least, that is what happened to me.

Fear left me. An odd peace came over me. The blade seemed no more than a toy. And my stomach growled. It was empty.

I turned my head. The rats had left some food on the plate. I reached for it. I put it to my lips and was about to eat it.

Then I paused. An idea had come to

me. An idea that made me forget my hunger.

My idea filled me with a new feeling. The feeling was foolish. But I could not deny it. I was starving for it.

It was a feeling of hope. Of joy, almost. Yet what business did I have with hope?

My idea came from the sight of the blade. It was very close now. Its sweep was now very wide—thirty feet or more. I could feel a breeze from it. I could imagine it cutting into my rough robe. Back and forth. Again and again.

But first it had to slice through the leather strap. The strap that tied me down.

As I said, it was a single strap. Wound around and around me. If it was cut, I could free myself. I had a chance, anyway. A hope.

I had to time it just right. I would grab the strap the moment it was cut. I would pull at it. It would come away from my body. I would roll away from the blade.

Again the blade swept down. It passed six inches from my chest.

My heart beat faster. My free hand tensed. Then another thought struck me. It made my stomach sink.

The blade swept down again. A little closer.

I raised my head. I looked at my chest.

It was as I feared.

There was a gap in the leather bandage around me. A gap right over my chest. The blade would not slice through the strap. Just through my robe. Then through my skin.

The Inquisition had thought of everything.

Again the blade swept down. Still closer. It should have brought fresh fear with it.

Instead it sparked anger in me. At the Inquisition. At the fiends who tormented me. Anger that was close to madness.

I would not let them win!

From this anger came one last mad plan.

I saw rats still coming out of the pit. They were angry, too. Angry and starving. They had been waiting for me down below. I had cheated them out of their meal.

They swarmed over the floor. They

licked the plate clean. And more kept coming.

I waved them away. They retreated. But only just out of reach of my arm. There they waited.

I realized why. I still held oily meat in my hand. They could smell it.

Again the blade swung down. It almost touched my robe. I smiled grimly.

Soon the rats would have what they wanted.

A feast.

The meat in my hand.

And me as well.

Then I put my plan in action.

I took the oily meat and rubbed it on the strap. On as much of the strap as I could touch.

Then I put my hand down by my side

and lay completely still. At first the rats were surprised by the change and drew back.

Then the boldest rat jumped on me. It sniffed the leather and began chewing at it.

Another rat came. And another.

Then a dam seemed to break. A flood of rats poured over me.

The sweeping blade kept them off my chest. But they covered all the rest of me. Hundreds of them. Hundreds upon hundreds. Heaps of them. Piling up. Fighting to get at me.

Rats nipped at my hands. Licked at my mouth. Shoved their snouts into my nose and ears. I shut my eyes to protect them. I felt rats crushing me with their weight. Smothering me with their stink.

But I felt something else, too.

I felt the strap loosening. Loosening more and more. As the rats tore at it.

I waited as long as I could. The pendulum came down again. To slice through my robe. And again to graze my skin. And yet again to draw blood.

I waited until the strap dropped away. And I could roll off the platform.

I lay on the floor. I shook off the rats. I watched the pendulum come down again. But this time it struck empty air.

I was free!

But my wild joy lasted only a moment.

I was free. But I was still in the hands of the Inquisition. I was sure it was watching me. I stood up on the stone floor of the prison. The hellish machine stopped.

The pendulum rose back to the

ceiling. Pulled by some invisible force. The Inquisition knew I had escaped the blade. They knew my every move.

The Inquisition had to be angry. Burning with rage. Even more than before. What would it do to me now?

I looked around me. What was the Inquisition's next move? I wanted to spot it early. So that I had more time to battle it.

Something seemed different in the dungeon. But I could not tell what. I looked even harder. I still could not spot the change.

One thing I did see, though. Where the light in the dungeon came from. There was an opening at the bottom of the metal walls. The light came through it.

I looked more closely at the opening.

It was half an inch wide. It ran around the entire room. It separated the walls from the floor.

I got down on my hands and knees. I tried to see through the opening. I wanted to learn what made the light. But I had no luck. Finally, I gave up trying.

I got to my feet. I saw that the dungeon was even more different. And now I could see what that difference was.

As I said, there were paintings on the walls. Demons and other monsters. Their colors had been dull and faded before. Now they were bright. And getting even brighter. Their very eyes seemed to be blazing with a gleam of fire. Blazing as they looked at me from a thousand directions.

I realized something else, too. It was

warmer in the dungeon. Sweat was pouring from me.

There was a new odor as well. I wondered what it was. Then I knew. The smell of heated iron.

Now I knew what made the light in the dungeon. The light that came through the opening. It was fire. Fire burning behind the walls. And now the Inquisition had added fuel to it. It was burning higher. Hotter.

The metal walls were glowing. I could feel their scorching heat.

I stepped back. Back from the rising heat. Back to the edge of the deadly pit. The cool, damp air from it actually felt good.

I turned my sweating face toward it. I looked down. The glare from the hot roof made it possible to see deep within the pit. I saw water gleaming far below. And the glowing eyes of countless rats. All waiting for me.

I screamed and buried my face in my hands. I could not stop myself from shaking. I could not keep tears from my eyes. I drew back from the edge of that horror as far as I could. But I could not go as far as before.

The dungeon was not only smaller. Its shape was different. It was no longer a perfect square. It was folding in on itself. Like a cardboard box being pushed flat.

The walls were moving! They were closing in on me!

I saw the glowing metal coming closer and closer. There was a low rumbling sound. The sound of a machine pushed to its limits. The Inquisition was eager for my death now. It was wasting no time. It was not going to make me suffer for hours. My death would be soon. And certain. And terrible.

I had to step back from the glowing metal. Back step by step. Back toward the edge of the pit.

Until I could go back no farther.

I stood at the edge of the pit. My back was toward it. I tried to hold my ground—my last little bit of ground. Any death but the pit! But the wall facing me was so close. The heat was so intense.

My face felt as if it were on fire. I could no longer stand it. My feet were slipping over the edge. I began to fall. I shut my eyes. My mouth opened. I gave one long last scream of despair. . . .

It died in the air. I felt a hand grabbing my arm as I fell.

I heard a voice saying my name. And other voices behind it. There was a loud blast of many trumpets.

I opened my eyes. The hot walls had pulled back. A man in uniform held me upright. It was he who had saved me.

I knew the uniform. It was French.

I knew the man. General Lasalle.

The French army had entered Toledo. The Inquisition was in the hands of its enemies.

Edgar Allan Poe was born in Boston, Massachusetts, in 1809. Raised by his uncle, who wanted Edgar to become a lawyer, Poe instead was drawn to a literary life. He worked as a magazine editor and critic while pursuing his writing career. His poems and criticism were greatly respected during his lifetime. However, today he is most famous for his dramatic tales of horror, filled with the strange and terrible, which continue to hold readers under their spell. Poe died at the age of forty in Baltimore, Maryland.

Les Martin has adapted *Oliver Twist* and *The Time Machine*, as well as *Edgar Allan Poe's Tales of Terror*, for the Stepping Stones series. He also writes original action and adventure stories for young readers. An avid tennis player, he lives in New York City.

**If you liked these scary stories,
you won't want to miss . . .**

The
Phantom
of the
Opera

by Gaston Leroux
adapted by Kate McMullan

I crept up a secret passage behind Box Five. I whispered to the managers. "Carlotta is singing tonight to bring down the lights!"

The managers looked around. Who had spoken? Then they looked up. The huge chandelier that hung over the hall was swaying back and forth. Back and forth. Faster and faster. And then . . . Crash! It fell!

"A little present from the Opera Ghost!" I howled.

FRANKENSTEIN

by **Mary Shelley**
adapted by **Larry Weinberg**

1 had to make other parts of the creature myself. He was going to be big. Eight feet tall! And stronger than any man or woman on earth.

At last I was ready. It was a cold and gloomy night in November. The room was dark when I went in. The creature lay on the table. It was a thing of death. But soon it would have life!

Dracula

BY BRAM STOKER
ADAPTED BY STEPHANIE SPINNER

That night Jonathan was shaving in his room. He used a small mirror that he had brought from England. There were no mirrors in the castle.

He heard someone behind him. It was the Count. But the Count did not appear in Jonathan's mirror. Jonathan turned white. A terrible thought came to him. The Count was not human!